© 1994 Geddes & Grosset Ltd
Published by Geddes & Grosset Ltd,
New Lanark, Scotland.

ISBN 1 85534 573 0

Printed and bound in Slovenia.

Jack and the Beanstalk

Retold by Judy Hamilton
Illustrated by Lindsay Duff

Tarantula Books

L ong ago, in a small country village, there lived a boy called Jack with his mother. Jack's father had died many years before, and Jack and his mother were very poor. Jack helped his mother to look after their small plot of land and their few animals, but one by one the animals died, until there was only one cow left. Weeds grew in the garden and the vegetables no longer grew strong and healthy. One day Jack's mother went to milk the cow and found that the cow could no longer produce any milk. It was too old.

"Jack, the cow is no use to us now," she said. "You must take her to market and sell her. Try to get a good price for her. We need money to buy food."

Jack set off for market early the next morning. It was a lovely day and Jack sauntered slowly along the road. The cow ambled along behind. Halfway to market, they met a travelling man who was resting by the side of the road.

"On your way to market are you, young fellow?" asked the man.

"Yes," said Jack, "I must sell my cow."

"I'll take the cow in exchange for these magic beans," said the man. He showed Jack the beans.

"Plant these in your garden, and amazing things will happen, you'll see!"

The magic beans sounded very exciting. Jack handed the cow's leading rope to the traveller, took the beans, and set off for home.

Jack's mother was angry when he got home.

"You stupid boy!" she cried tearfully. "These beans are no use! They won't even grow!"

She threw them out of the window.

"Now we shall probably starve!"

Jack went to bed hungry and unhappy.

Next morning he was hungrier than ever. There was no food in the house so he went out into the garden to see what he could find. But when he opened the back door he gasped as he caught sight of the biggest beanstalk that he had ever seen, stretching high into the sky.

"I wonder how high this beanstalk reaches," thought Jack and he began to climb.

All day long, Jack climbed. He was very tired but he did not stop. Up he went, higher than the highest mountain. When Jack at last reached the top it was dark. A road stretched ahead of him in the blackness, and he started off to see where it would lead. He had not gone far, when he came to a huge castle. He knocked on the great door and a woman answered.

"I'm tired and hungry," said Jack. "May I rest here and have some food?"

The woman ushered him into a huge kitchen. Two enormous pots were bubbling on a stove.

"You may have some food," said the woman, "but when my husband the giant comes home, run for your life. He eats boys like you!"

Jack had a delicious meal, but he had hardly finished when he heard the thunder of giant footsteps. He ran to hide in a giant big empty copper pot.

"**Fee, foh, fi, fum!**" roared the giant. "I smell the blood of an Englishman!"

"Nonsense, dear," insisted his wife. "Your hunger is making you imagine things."

She set an enormous plate of food in front of him and he began to eat very noisily. He finished his meal with a great big belch.

"Wife!" he bellowed, "Bring my money!"

Jack carefully lifted the lid of the pot and saw the giant's wife stagger in, carrying several big bags of gold. The giant emptied the gold into a gleaming mountain on the table.

The giant's wife went to bed and Jack watched the giant count the coins one by one. When he had finished, he put them back in the bags, laid his head on his arms, and went to sleep.

The snoring of the giant shook the furniture and rattled the pots. Silently, Jack climbed out of his pot and crept up to the table. Then he lifted three of the bags of gold from the table and slipped out of the great kitchen and into the hall.

Jack reached up and turned the giant-sized key in the front door. He slid out and ran as fast as he could along the road to the beanstalk.

His mother, anxiously waiting at home, got a wonderful surprise when she saw what he had brought.

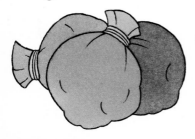

Jack and his mother had enough gold to keep them living comfortably for the rest of their lives. With the house in good repair, fine clothes to wear and plenty of food, Jack should have settled down, but he was restless for another adventure.

One morning he began to climb the beanstalk again. When he finally reached the top he headed straight for the giant's house. The giant's wife looked frightened when she answered the door.

"You must not come in!" she cried. "My husband will find you and eat you for sure!"

But Jack looked so tired that she took pity on him, and let him into the kitchen for a meal.

He had hardly finished eating when he heard the giant's roar and ran to hide.

"**Fee, foh, fi, fum!** I *can* smell an Englishman! If he was the one who robbed me then I shall eat him slowly, bit by bit!"

"Don't be silly, dear," his wife spoke gently. "It's only the sausages for supper that you can smell."

The giant grunted and sat down at the table. He shovelled the steaming piles of food into his mouth and slurped his ale noisily.

When he had finished he called his wife. "Woman, bring me my hen!"

The giant's wife brought the hen to the table, then bade the giant goodnight.

The giant turned to the hen and roared;

"Lay, hen, lay!"

Jack watched the hen give a squawk, flutter its wings and deposit a shining golden egg on the table. Again the giant gave the command and again the hen laid a golden egg. The hen carried on laying to the giant's commands until a great pile of eggs had been laid. Then the giant closed his eyes and dozed off to sleep. Jack sneaked up to the table and grabbed the hen. With one hand holding her beak shut to keep her quiet, he ran to the door.

When Jack reached the foot of the beanstalk next morning he presented the hen to his mother. They would now be very wealthy indeed.

But Jack's mother had been very afraid while he was up the beanstalk and now she told him why.

"Jack, when you were young, your father went to market one day and never came back," she explained. "Weeks later, a travelling man came and told me that he had found the giant's kingdom with your father. The giant saw your father and ate him up. Jack, this must be the giant that you have been stealing from! Don't go back!"

But Jack would not listen to her. He vowed to avenge his father's death. He made up his mind to go up the beanstalk one last time.

The giant's wife was terrified, but at last let Jack into the castle. Jack had no time to eat before the giant came back.

"Fee, foh, fi, fum!" the giant bellowed, "*This* time I *can* smell an Englishman!"

The giant's wife once again calmed him and gave him his dinner. When he had finished, he swept his plate aside and bellowed,

"Wife! Bring me my golden harp!"

When the harp was brought before him, the giant commanded,

"Play, harp, play!"

Song after song, the harp entertained the giant until he commanded it to stop. Then the giant went to sleep. Jack leapt out and snatched the harp. But the harp sounded the alarm.

"Help, master, help!" it cried.

With a roar, the giant woke up.

"Fee, foh, fi, fum!" he bellowed. "I'm going to eat you–here I come!"

Jack ran like the wind, carrying the screeching harp, with the giant lumbering after him. Jack reached the beanstalk first and began to scramble down. When he felt the beanstalk shake with the weight of the giant coming after him, he went faster. He slithered to the bottom, ran to the house and grabbed his axe. The giant's great foot was appearing through the clouds on the swaying beanstalk. Jack swung the axe and hit the beanstalk again and again. The beanstalk creaked then broke in two.

"That is for my father!" shouted Jack as the giant fell to earth with a tremendous crash.

Jack's adventures were over, and he had no need to fear the giant again.